HOCKEY MY HERO
A Jimmy Sprinkles Adventure

By Scott Rowsick
Illustrated by
Arnold Hullenbaugh

Dedicated to Henry and Tiger Lilly
We love you, always.

I'm up bright and early to start the day
Going to practice my skills and play
But first to the kitchen to sit and eat
Then it's off to the rink to skate and
compete!

Then I get my bag
And grab my sticks
Make sure it's
all there
And everything fits!

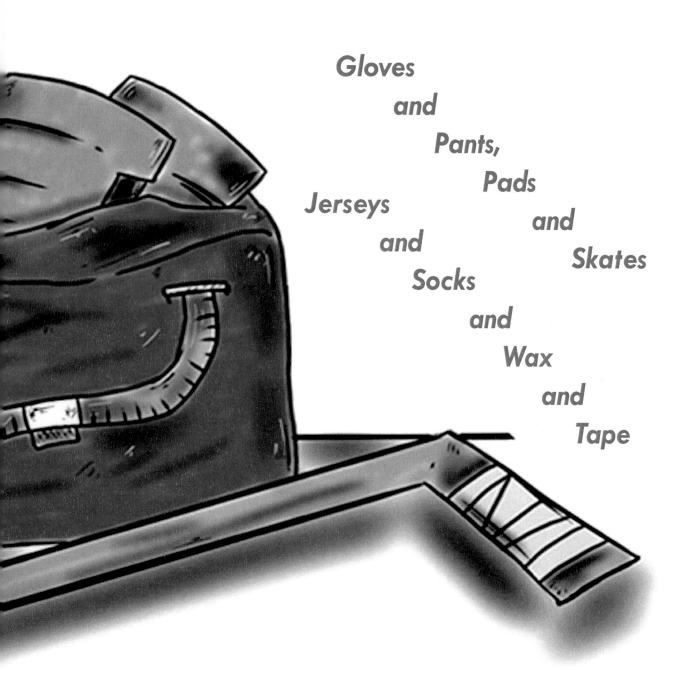

Gloves
and
Pants,
Pads
and
Skates
Jerseys
and
Socks
and
Wax
and
Tape

Up the ice
and
Down the boards
I'll skate,
I'll pass
I'll shoot
I'll Score!

I get to the rink
And say "Hi!" to the team
They are my friends,
we have the same dream

We want to play in the
national league
And win the cup they call
Stanley!

Into the locker room to put on my gear

Safety's important, we play with no fear

Strap it all on from helmet to socks

And put on my jersey with the sign that says **"STOP"**

We must keep in mind
The rules of the game

Don't want to
spend any
time in the
box

In there you feel two
minutes of shame

And hope that your goalie
makes all the stops!

No hooking, no holding,
no boarding in play

No charging, no fighting
allowed on the ice

We play hard
to win, but in
the right way

And keep our heads up
and sticks on the ice

I can't wait to get on the rink
The Zamboni goes 'round and 'round
I wave to my dad and then I think
I cannot wait to make him proud!

Here we go now, it's time to play
Coach wishes us all good luck
I'm ready to score, ready to skate
The referee drops the puck!

I take the puck and I skate and I skate
And I look for a lane to pass
My eyes find my two line mates
And we skate in the zone so *fast!*

I snap one on goal and we skate to the net
The puck gets kicked to the slot
Get to the slot and there's a pretty safe bet
You'll get a pretty good chance at a pretty
good shot!

Just as I get there, just like I
thought
The puck lands *right* *on* *my* *stick!*

I pick up my head just like I was
taught
And I *pick* *a* *good* *spot* for my shot

The puck goes *flying* into the goal!
I raise my hands in the air

"Yay!" We all scream, and then we huddle
To celebrate the lead we now share

We scored a few more by the end of the game

4 - to - **1**
was the final score!

And our goalie
made so many
good saves

It's time for
celebrations galore!

Back to the locker room to laugh with my friends
To celebrate and have a good time

Keep all my gear on, the fun doesn't end
I'm practicing now with a *hero* *of* *mine*

It's **daddy** who taught me all of the rules
He **loves** to watch me skate

He loves me with all of his heart and says
That I am **going** to be great!

It's not always easy when you're playing the game
And sometimes it downright *stinks!*

But if you *work really hard*, you get good
then great
It's all in the way that you think!

I skate just as fast as I can
And my Daddy sees me rush by

"*You skate like the wind!*"
Daddy said and then he grinned
And then I started to smile

These are the best of times
My spirits are *high!* And my fears are *zero!*

I can't help but smile so bright
When I play...

HOCKEY WITH MY HERO

...the end.

Printed in the United States of America

First Printing, 2016

ISBN 978-0-692-77305-5

Pastime Publications, LLC
1303 Waterfront Dr. Ste. 102
Virginia Beach, VA 23451

www.pastimepublicationsllc.com

Made in the USA
San Bernardino, CA
18 September 2016